MOLE'S HARVEST MOON

Judi Abbot

PICTURE CORGI

The leaves were turning golden brown and
falling from the trees, and the wind was getting chilly
as six friends were planning a harvest feast.

"Come back to my home,"
said Mole. "Let's have the feast there!"
"Perfect!" agreed Rabbit.

"Hurray!"

shouted Bear.

"What a treat!"

"I'll cook," said Duck. "We could have delicious buttered corn-on-the-cob, stuffed mushrooms and a creamy pumpkin soup."

"And I can make my special apple, pear and berry pie," said Dog.

"But, Mole," said Mouse, sounding a little worried. "Do we have all the ingredients?"

"Ah. Well, I have all the main ingredients
in my kitchen cupboard," said Mole.
"But we will also need some things from the
other side of the Whispering Woods."

"Some of us should stay here to start
getting the feast ready," said Duck.
So Bear, Mouse and Rabbit agreed to go
and gather the other things they needed.

They set off with some baskets and a huge sack to carry it all home.
"Try to get back before dark," called Mole.
"But if night falls then just look out for the **harvest moon**.
It will guide you right back to my home in the hill."

The Whispering Woods were full of
wild mushrooms - perfect for the feast.
"These woods aren't so frightening," said Bear.
"That's because it's daytime," answered Rabbit.
"Some say there's a gang of wicked **weasels**
that stalk the woods by night."

Tri**p**

"Oh dear, oh dear!"
squeaked Mouse.
"We don't have long until nightfall."
In his worry he tripped over a tree root,
spilling mushrooms everywhere.
"Oh, Mouse," sighed Bear and Rabbit.

Further on, the friends found delicious raspberries and blackberries growing in a hedgerow at the far side of the woods.

"It's going to get dark soon, we must
hurry!" squeaked Mouse.
"Don't worry, Mouse," smiled Bear. "Mole
promised us that, even if it gets dark, the light
from the harvest moon will lead us home."

But Mouse was still worried. The sky was getting darker
and so the friends hurried on.

Soon they reached an orchard filled with delicious-looking
apples and a little further on were more trees full of juicy pears.
They chose the ripest fruit to go with the berries for Dog's special pie.

"Maybe we should go back now," said Rabbit,
looking up at the sky. "It really is getting dark."
"And the sky is so cloudy that we may not be able
to see the harvest moon," worried Mouse.
"Well, the last ingredients are just in the next field," said Bear.

Next to the orchard they found a field of sweetcorn
and gigantic orange pumpkins.
"Perfect!" said Bear as he filled the big sack.
"And look, some of the pumpkins have already
been carved and decorated."

Suddenly ...

"Eeeeeeeeeeeeeeeeeek!!"

shrieked Mouse as a dark shadow loomed over him.
"It's the wicked weasels!"

But it was only a scarecrow.
"Oh, Mouse!" said Bear. Rabbit gave Mouse a hug to calm him down.
"Now let's hurry back to Mole's house," said Rabbit.

But as they followed their steps back through the woods they realised that they were being followed.

Three figures were slowly creeping along the path behind them.

"Yikes!" squeaked Mouse. "I think we'd better hurry."

But the quicker the friends walked, the quicker the figures followed. As they made their way along the windy path, darkness had fallen in the Whispering Woods. Just then the cloud cleared, and by the light of the harvest moon, the friends could see exactly who the mysterious strangers were.

It was the **wicked weasels** giving chase!
The friends rushed deeper into the woods just
as the cloud shrouded everything in darkness again.

Luckily the weasels couldn't see
where the friends had gone ...

"Quick, I have a plan,"
whispered Rabbit.
And they hurried to get ready.

Suddenly, the harvest moon came out from behind a
cloud and shone brightly, showing the weasels
something very unexpected indeed ...

It was a huge, ghostly, frightening figure with
a horrible grin on its face. It glowed as it loomed
over the terrified weasels.

"Aaaaaargh!,"

the weasels cried,
and they fled as fast as they could.

But it was only Bear, Mouse and Rabbit in disguise!
They pulled off the sack and the pumpkin head, and they
laughed and laughed at how they'd tricked the wicked weasels.
Then they quickly gathered up the food that they'd carefully
stored and hurried on their way.

And as they looked up – there it was
the shining harvest moon, hanging in the sky
just above Mole's home in the hill.

As the friends reached Mole's hill,
Mole, Dog and Duck rushed out.
"We've been so worried about you", cried Duck.
"There's a terrible monster in the wood."
"A monster?" said Mouse. "There wasn't
a monster. Just a band of wicked weasels."

"Wicked weasels?" asked Mole. And then he smiled.
And then his smile turned into a chuckle.
"What's so funny?" said Bear, crossly.
"I think I know what's happened," said Mole.
"Come with me."

And there in Mole's living room, looking
rather shaken, were three weary weasels.
"Meet my friends, the weasels," said Mole. "We were worried,
so I sent them to help you home – they know the woods so well.
But they ran back in terror saying they'd seen a monster!"

While Duck, Dog and Mole finished preparing the sumptuous feast, Rabbit and Mouse took turns in telling the whole story.

"…and, just as you said, Mole,
the light from the harvest moon helped us find home,"
finished Rabbit, giving him a big hug.

Throughout that evening, in front of the roaring fire,
the six friends and the friendly weasels, full from their
harvest feast, laughed, played games and told stories
together. And through the window, silently shimmering
above them all, shone the brilliant, bright harvest moon.